GOOD KING WENCESLAS
A TRADITIONAL TALE

It was midnight on Christmas Eve, and King Wenceslas was busy wrapping presents for everyone in the castle. For his dear Queen, he wrapped a pair of silver skates. For Albert, his page, he wrapped a very difficult jigsaw puzzle. The footmen were given penknives, nuts and marzipan, and for the cooks there were china ornaments and talcum powder. And everyone had a tangerine each.

When he had finished his wrapping, the King tiptoed around the castle, hanging a stocking at the end of each bed.

He had just enough time to hang the last stocking before the whole castle began to wake up.

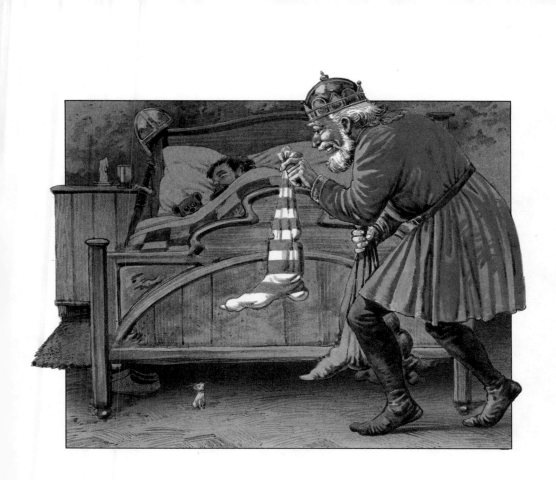

King Wenceslas tumbled into bed, exhausted after his night's work. The Queen, page, footmen and cooks, full of excitement, tore open their packages. There was brightly-colored paper and string scattered everywhere as they admired their gifts.

What a commotion there was in the kitchen – banging and chopping and scraping and basting. The table was laden with roast potatoes, plum pudding, crème caramel and lime dessert, guinea-fowl and turkey to be prepared for the feast.

Albert, having nothing much to do while the King slept, was busy tasting each dish and looking forward to his Christmas dinner.

Meanwhile King Wenceslas snored on and on. The Queen came in, kissed him, and gave him a pair of slippers embroidered with his initials. He mumbled, "Charming, my dear," and went right back to sleep. Albert, tiring of his hard work in the kitchen, came in and gave him a goldfish he had won at the summer fair. King Wenceslas murmured, "Delightful, my boy," and went back to sleep again.

While King Wenceslas slept, the Queen, Albert, the court and guests from far and wide ate their sumptuous Christmas dinner.

Glasses were filled and refilled, and plates were piled high with delicious morsels. And then the entertainment began. The King of France even danced the tango with his pet bear!

A bard from a far-off land recited a long poem, and everyone began to feel very weary. The singing, laughter and shrieks of excitement died away. The whole party nodded quietly in their seats, as the candles flickered softly. Outside the darkness fell, where silent snow had already fallen.

King Wenceslas woke refreshed from his sleep. He stretched, jumped out of bed and pushed his feet into his new slippers. Then he leaned out the bedroom window, sniffing the frosty air with pleasure.

Down below he spied an old man collecting firewood. "I wonder who that can be, wandering about outside on a night like this?" thought the King. He went to look for Albert, who was still snoozing peacefully in the dining hall.

King Wenceslas shook his page gently by the shoulder. "Wake up, my boy, I need your help," he whispered.

Albert rubbed his eyes, yawning and protesting. "Oh, sire, I've eaten too much. I feel so sleepy."

"Come, my boy, we've got work to do. But first, tell me — do you know who that old man might be I've just seen outside the castle?"

"Oh, yes, sire. He lives at the bottom of the mountain. He often comes here looking for firewood."

"Hmm. Albert, fetch me as many pine logs as you can carry," said King Wenceslas suddenly. While Albert was collecting the wood, King Wenceslas went around the table, filling a basket with chunks of meat and bottles of wine.

When Albert returned he was staggering under a pile of logs. "Put on your warmest cloak," King Wenceslas told him. "We're off to visit our friend at the bottom of the mountain and give him a surprise."

"But, sire! That's miles away and it's freezing outside!" cried Albert.

"Just remember," the King answered kindly, "not everyone has the splendid Christmas that you have, or a warm castle to live in."

And off they tramped in the snow.

When they reached the old man's house, they laid all their supplies outside the door.

"There," said King Wenceslas. "Now at least he'll have some Christmas dinner, and enough wood to last for a few days."

Albert followed King Wenceslas back to the castle. As he walked he had the strangest feeling. Each time he stood in his master's footprints in the snow, his body tingled all over with warmth as though it was the finest summer's day.

"I wonder if anyone would believe me if I told them," thought Albert. "No," he decided, "they'd probably just laugh at me." And he snuggled up contentedly inside his cloak as the lights of the castle came into view.

Good King Wenceslas is based upon a Christmas carol written in the 19th century. The carol praises the virtues of Wenceslas I, who ruled Bohemia (Czechoslovakia) from 921 to 929. At the time he took the throne, Christian and non-Christian factions were in conflict. Wenceslas had been raised as a Christian, and he spread his faith with zeal. His devotion angered non-Christian nobles, who plotted to kill him in 929. He was murdered by his brother Boleslav on the church steps as he was on his way to mass.